# OWL AT HOME

## by ARNOLD LOBEL

An I CAN READ Book®

HarperCollins*Publishers*

*For Grandma*

HarperCollins®, ☼®, and I Can Read Book® are trademarks of HarperCollins Publishers.

Library of Congress Catalog Card Number: 74-2630
ISBN-10: 0-06-023949-2 (lib. bdg.) — ISBN-13: 978-0-06-023949-7 (lib. bdg.)
ISBN-10: 0-06-444034-6 (pbk.) — ISBN-13: 978-0-06-444034-9 (pbk.)

19  20  SCP  20  19  18
❖

# CONTENTS

# THE GUEST

Owl was at home.
"How good it feels
to be sitting
by this fire," said Owl.
"It is so cold
and snowy outside."
Owl was eating
buttered toast
and hot pea soup
for supper.

Owl heard a loud sound

at the front door.

"Who is out there,

banging and pounding

at my door

on a night like this?"

he said.

Owl opened the door.

No one was there.

Only the snow

and the wind.

Owl sat near the fire again.

There was another loud noise
at the door.

"Who can it be," said Owl,

"knocking and thumping

at my door on a night like this?"

Owl opened the door.

No one was there.

Only the snow

and the cold.

"The poor old winter

is knocking at my door,"

said Owl.

"Perhaps it wants to sit

by the fire.

Well, I will be kind

and let the winter come in."

Owl opened the door very wide.

"Come in, Winter,"

said Owl.

"Come in and warm yourself

for a while."

Winter came into the house.

It came in very fast.

A cold wind

pushed Owl against the wall.

10

Winter ran around the room.

It blew out the fire

in the fireplace.

The snow whirled

up the stairs

and whooshed down the hallway.

"Winter!" cried Owl.

"You are my guest.

This is no way to behave!"

But Winter did not listen.

It made the window shades

flap and shiver.

It turned the pea soup

into hard, green ice.

Winter went into all the rooms
of Owl's house.

Soon everything

was covered with snow.

"You must go, Winter!"

shouted Owl.

"Go away, right now!"

The wind blew

around and around.

Then Winter rushed out

and slammed the front door.

"Good-bye," called Owl,

"and do not come back!"

Owl made a new fire

in the fireplace.

The room became

warm again.

The snow melted away.

The hard, green ice

turned back

into soft pea soup.

Owl sat down in his chair

and quietly

finished his supper.

# STRANGE BUMPS

Owl was in bed.

"It is time

to blow out the candle

and go to sleep,"

he said with a yawn.

Then Owl saw two bumps

under his blanket

at the bottom of his bed.

"What can those strange bumps

be?" asked Owl.

Owl lifted up the blanket.

He looked down into the bed.

All he could see was darkness.

Owl tried to sleep,

but he could not.

"What if those

two strange bumps

grow bigger and bigger

while I am asleep?"

said Owl.

"That would not be pleasant."

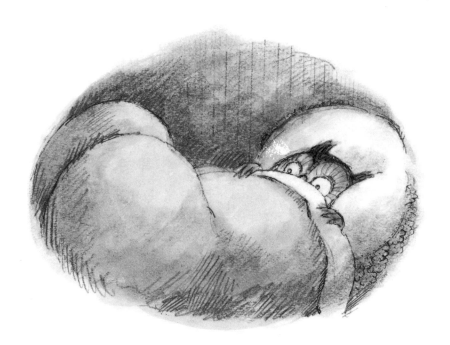

Owl moved his right foot
up and down.
The bump on the right
moved up and down.
"One of those bumps
is moving!" said Owl.
Owl moved his left foot
up and down.
The bump
on the left
moved up and down.
"The other bump is moving!"
cried Owl.

Owl pulled

all of the covers

off his bed.

The bumps were gone.

All Owl could see

at the bottom of the bed

were his own two feet.

"But now I am cold,"

said Owl.

"I will cover myself

with the blankets again."

As soon as he did,

he saw the same two bumps.

"Those bumps are back!"

shouted Owl.

"Bumps, bumps, bumps!

I will never sleep tonight!"

Owl jumped

up and down

on top of his bed.

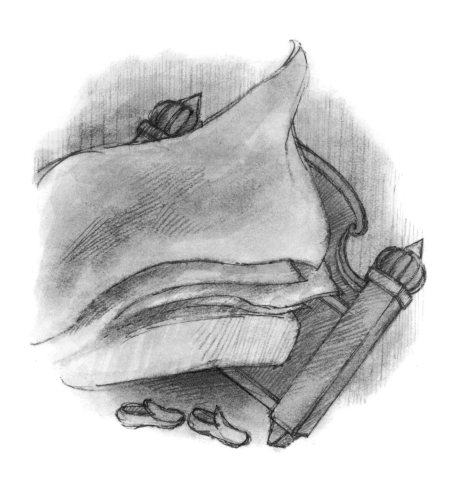

"Where are you?

What are you?" he cried.

With a crash and a bang

the bed came falling down.

Owl ran

down the stairs.

He sat in his chair

near the fire.

"I will let those two strange bumps

sit on my bed

all by themselves,"

said Owl.

"Let them grow

as big as they wish.

I will sleep right here

where I am safe."

And that is what he did.

# TEAR-WATER TEA

Owl took the kettle
out of the cupboard.
"Tonight I will make
tear-water tea," he said.
He put the kettle on his lap.
"Now," said Owl,
"I will begin."
Owl sat very still.
He began to think of
things that were sad.

"Chairs with broken legs,"
said Owl.
His eyes
began to water.

"Songs that cannot be sung,"
said Owl,
"because the words
have been forgotten."

Owl began to cry.
A large tear
rolled down
and dropped
into the kettle.

"Spoons that have fallen
behind the stove
and are never seen again,"
said Owl.

More tears dropped down
into the kettle.

33

"Books that cannot
be read," said Owl,
"because some of the pages
have been torn out."

"Clocks that have stopped,"
said Owl,
"with no one near
to wind them up."

Owl was crying.
Many large tears
dropped into the kettle.
"Mornings nobody saw
because everybody
was sleeping,"
sobbed Owl.

"Mashed potatoes
left on a plate," he cried,
"because no one
wanted to eat them.
And pencils
that are too short to use."

Owl thought about
many other sad things.
He cried and cried.

Soon the kettle

was all filled up

with tears.

"There," said Owl.

"That does it!"

Owl stopped crying.

He put the kettle

on the stove

to boil for tea.

Owl felt happy
as he filled his cup.
"It tastes
a little bit salty,"
he said,
"but tear-water tea
is always very good."

# UPSTAIRS AND DOWNSTAIRS

Owl's house had an upstairs
and a downstairs.
There were twenty steps
on the stairway.
Some of the time
Owl was upstairs
in his bedroom.
At other times
Owl was downstairs
in his living room.

When Owl was downstairs

he said, "I wonder

how my upstairs is?"

When Owl was upstairs

he said, "I wonder

how my downstairs

is getting along?

I am always missing

one place or the other.

There must be a way," said Owl,

"to be upstairs

and to be downstairs

at the same time."

"Perhaps if I run
very very fast,
I can be
in both places at once."
Owl ran up
the stairs.
"I am up," he said.

Owl ran down the stairs.
"I am down,"
he said.

Owl ran
up and down
the stairs
faster and faster.
"Owl!" he cried.
"Are you downstairs?"
There was no answer.
"No," said Owl.
"I am not downstairs
because I am upstairs.
I am not running fast enough."

"Owl!" he shouted.

"Are you upstairs?"

There was no answer.

"No," said Owl.

"I am not upstairs

because I am downstairs.

I must run even faster."

"Faster, faster, faster!"

cried Owl.

Owl ran upstairs

and downstairs

all evening.

But he could not be

in both places at once.

"When I am up," said Owl,

"I am not down.

When I am down

I am not up.

All I am is very tired!"

Owl sat down to rest.

He sat on the tenth step

because it was a place

that was

right in the middle.

# OWL AND THE MOON

One night

Owl went down

to the seashore.

He sat on a large rock

and looked out at the waves.

Everything was dark.

Then a small tip

of the moon

came up

over the edge of the sea.

Owl watched the moon.

It climbed higher and higher
into the sky.

Soon the whole, round moon
was shining.

Owl sat on the rock
and looked up at the moon
for a long time.

"If I am looking
at you, moon,
then you must be
looking back at me.
We must be
very good friends."

The moon did not answer,

but Owl said,

"I will come back

and see you again, moon.

But now I must go home."

Owl walked down the path.

He looked up at the sky.

The moon was still there.

It was following him.

"No, no, moon," said Owl.
"It is kind of you
to light my way.
But you must stay up
over the sea
where you look so fine."
Owl walked on a little farther.
He looked at the sky again.

There was the moon
coming right along with him.
"Dear moon," said Owl,
"you really must not
come home with me.
My house is small.
You would not fit
through the door.
And I have nothing
to give you for supper."

Owl kept on walking.

The moon

sailed after him

over the tops of the trees.

"Moon," said Owl,

"I think that

you do not hear me."

Owl climbed

to the top of a hill.

He shouted

as loudly as he could,

"Good-bye, moon!"

The moon went behind some clouds.

Owl looked and looked.

The moon was gone.

"It is always

a little sad

to say good-bye to a friend,"

said Owl.

Owl came home.

He put on his pajamas
and went to bed.

The room was very dark.

Owl was still feeling sad.

All at once,

Owl's bedroom

was filled with silver light.

Owl looked out of the window.

The moon was coming

from behind the clouds.

"Moon, you have followed me

all the way home.

What a good, round friend

you are!" said Owl.

Then Owl put his head
on the pillow
and closed his eyes.
The moon was shining
down through the window.
Owl did not
feel sad at all.